Sam's Sneaker Squares

by Nat Gabriel
Illustrated by Ron Fritz

The Kane Press
New York

Book Design/Art Direction: Roberta Pressel

Library of Congress Cataloging-in-Publication Data

Gabriel, Nat.
    Sam's sneaker squares by Nat Gabriel ; illustrated by Ron Fritz.
      p.   cm. — (Math matters.)
    Summary: With his brother's help, Sam figures out how to measure the size of the lawns he mows.
    ISBN 1-57565-114-9 (pbk. : alk. paper)
    [1. Area measurement—Fiction.] I. Fritz, Ronald, ill. II. Title. III. Series.
  PZ7.G1156 Sam 2002
  [E]—dc21
2001038803   CIP
                                                                                                           AC

10 9 8 7 6 5 4 3 2 1

First published in the United States of America in 2002 by The Kane Press.
Printed in Hong Kong.

I thought mowing lawns would be easy.
The first one was. But the next one
seemed to take forever! I had to finish it,
though. Otherwise I wouldn't get paid.
And no money would mean no new bike.

"Oh, Sam! I just washed the floor!"
said Mom.

I looked down. "Whoops. Sorry, Mom.
I guess I forgot to wipe my feet," I said.

"Let me guess," said my older brother,
Dave. "Was your mind somewhere else?
Like on another *planet* maybe?"

"Don't tease your brother, Dave," said Mom. "He can't help it if—"

"He's a deep thinker," said Dave.

"That's right," Mom said. "The world needs deep thinkers like our Sam."

My brother rolled his eyes.

"So, what were you thinking about, honey?" Mom asked.

"Mr. Hill's backyard," I said.

"Wow, that's deep all right," said Dave.

"How much bigger do you think it is than Mrs. Green's yard?" I asked him.

"Why do you care?" Dave said.

"Because it took a lot longer to mow his lawn than hers," I said. "I told Mr. Hill that, but he said I was probably just tired from not drinking enough milk or something."

"I'm sure his lawn is a lot bigger than hers,"
I said. "I wish I could prove it. Then maybe
he'd pay me more."

"I could show you how," said Dave.

"Great," I said. "So . . . how?"

"What's in it for me?" Dave asked.

"I'll clear your dishes for a week," I offered.

Dave drew a rectangle on his napkin.
"Say this is a lawn," he said. "You measure
the two sides—the length and width. Then
you divide it into equal squares—like this."

"Then what?" I asked.
"You count up all the squares. The more
squares, the bigger the area."
"You mean the bigger the lawn?" I asked.
"You've got it!" said Dave.

I sort of got it and sort of didn't. How was I supposed to measure the lawn? With a ruler? That would take forever.

"But how am I supposed to—" I said.
Just then a horn honked. Dave grabbed his
jacket and headed out the door.

"Gotta go," he said.

"Wait!" I yelled, starting to run after him.

"Stop, Sam! My floor! Just look at it!"
cried Mom.

I'd been so busy talking to Dave, I'd
forgotten all about my muddy sneakers.
I looked at the footprints. And that's
when it hit me.

"Mom, you're a genius," I said. "You
were right. All I needed to do was just look
at the floor."

Mom scratched her head and went to
get the mop.

I took off my sneakers and hurried up to my room.

"Let's say this rug is Mrs. Green's lawn," I said to myself. I started walking down the long side of the rug. It took six steps to get across.

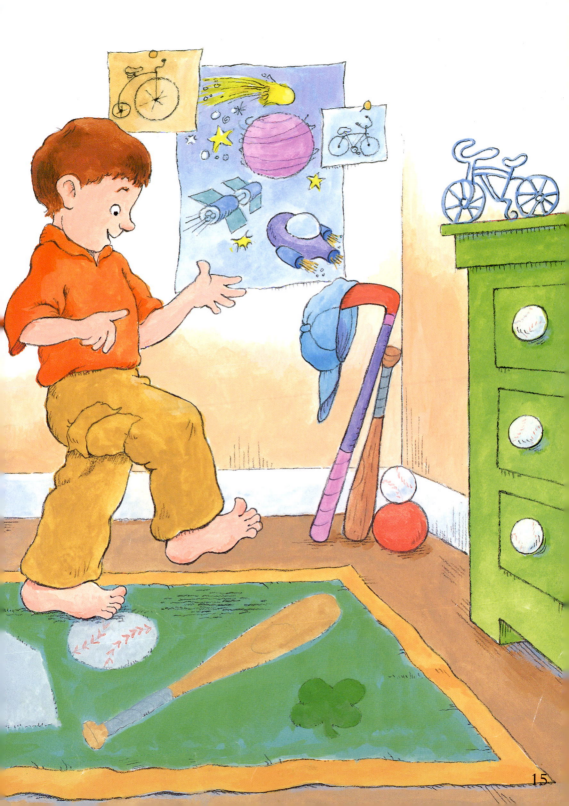

Then I turned and started walking down the short side of the rug. Three steps. Six steps across and three steps down.

"What on earth are you doing, Sam?"
Mom called from downstairs. "You sound
like an elephant."

"I'm measuring Mrs. Green's lawn!" I
called back.

Mom didn't answer, but I heard her start
coming up the stairs.

On a piece of paper I drew a rectangle. I drew six sneaker prints on one side, like the ones I'd made on Mom's clean floor. Then I put three more prints along the other side.

I divided the whole thing into squares.
Sneaker squares, I decided to call them.

"Did you say you're measuring a lawn?"
Mom said.

"Yeah, and it's 18 sneaker squares big,"
I said. "Isn't that cool?"

All day I practiced measuring. I measured the living room. Dad wasn't too thrilled.

I measured the den. Mom seemed glad when I was all done.

I measured every room in the house.
Boy, all that measuring made me hungry
and tired. So I had a snack. Then I took a
nap. Guess what?

I dreamed about sneaker squares! Everywhere I went people kept asking me to measure things.

"The parking lot, Sam!"

"The football field, Sam!"

"No, Sam. Measure ME!" I heard a strange voice behind me say.

I turned around. There stood a giant peanut butter and jelly sandwich. It smiled and began to chase me around the room, yelling—

"Sam! Sam!"

I opened my eyes. *Whew!* It was only my mother calling me, not a sandwich.

I was supposed to be at Mrs. Green's house mowing her lawn. I ran over there as fast as I could. But before I started mowing, I measured. Her lawn was twenty steps long and ten steps wide. Wow! This was easy. I made a grid and counted by tens.

"Your lawn is exactly 200 sneaker squares big," I said.

"That's nice, dear," said Mrs. Green.

She paid me, and I headed over to Mr. Hill's house.

"I don't think the grass has had a chance to grow much since this morning," Mr. Hill called out. "Come back next week, okay?"

"I'm not here to mow, I'm here to measure," I explained.

"One, two, three, four—" I said, taking sneaker steps along the edges of the yard.

"That looks like fun. Can I help?" asked Mr. Hill.

"No, thanks," I said. "Your feet are longer than mine. Your sneaker steps would be way too big."

Mr. Hill gave me that same look my mother always does.

When I had finished measuring, I gave Mr. Hill the news.

"The reason your yard takes longer to mow is that it's 160 sneaker squares bigger than Mrs. Green's," I told him.

"Are you sure?" he asked.

"I'm positive," I said. "So I'll have to charge you more."

"That's fair," he said. "But I still think you should drink more milk."

After I left Mr. Hill's, it hit me. "Wow," I thought. "If I can find even bigger lawns to mow, I can earn a lot more money. That bike could be mine in no time at all!"

I couldn't wait to tell everybody my idea. I ran all the way home.

"Guess what I'm going to do?" I said.

"I don't know," said my mother. "But I know what you forgot to do."

"Whoops!" I said, looking down at the floor. "I'm sorry, Mom! But wait till you hear *this*!"

AREA CHART

> The amount of space covered by a figure is called its **area**.

Area is measured in square units.

1 square unit

Sam says the area of each figure is 36 square units.
Is he right? How do you know?

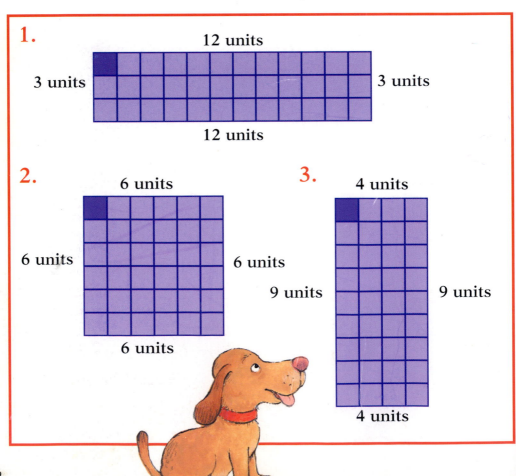

1.

12 units

3 units   3 units

12 units

2.

6 units

6 units   6 units

6 units

3.

4 units

9 units   9 units

4 units